FUGITIVE RED

FUGITIVE RED

KAREN DONOVAN

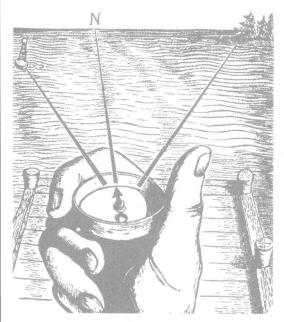

University of Massachusetts Press ❧ *Amherst*

Printed in the United States of America
LC 98–32203
ISBN 1–55849–199–6
Designed by Jack Harrison
Printed and bound by BookCrafters
Library of Congress Cataloging-in-Publication Data

Donovan, Karen, 1956–
Fugitive Red / Karen Donovan.
     p.   cm.
ISBN 1–55849–199–6 (pbk. : alk. paper)
I. Title
PS3554.O554F84   1999
811' .54—dc21   98–32203
                                   CIP

British Library Cataloguing in Publication data are available.

Asking what happens before the Big Bang is like asking for a point one mile north of the North Pole. The quantity that we measure as time had a beginning, but that does not mean spacetime has an edge, just as the surface of the Earth does not have an edge at the North Pole, or at least, so I am told; I have not been there myself.

— *Stephen W. Hawking*

Even angels long to look into these things.

— *1 Peter 1:12*

Acknowledgments

The author would like to thank the Alden B. Dow Creativity Center for a summer fellowship.

Grateful acknowledgment is also made to the following publications, where versions of these poems first appeared:

Field: "The Return of Fugitive Red"; "The Enthymeme in Perspective"

The Georgia Review: "Travel Silk"

Nimrod: "The Plumber's Begun to Notice"; "Nothing by Mouth"

Willow Springs: "Chemo"

Indiana Review: "Dissecting *Drosophila* with Marcie: Tucson, Arizona"; "The Fishway at Holyoke"

Southern Poetry Review: "The Scout Looks for Bee Purple"; "The Many Uses of Camouflage"; "Walking the Ouachita"

College English: "Dissipative Structures"; "Brief History of Peacetime"

Lines 15 and 16 of "Brief History of Peacetime" are borrowed from an essay by George Leonard called "The Warrior."

Contents

IV. Return

NAVIGATION

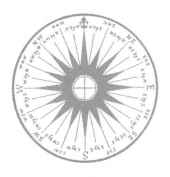

Dissecting *Drosophila* with Marcie: Tucson, Arizona

It's a familiar, luminous habit,
like turning a sock inside out,
except the sock is the head of a fruit fly larva.
You have to lop it off with tiny scissors.
Reversed, the pattern unravels
a backstage code for metamorphosis,
imaginal discs strung out under the lens like charms.
From each plate of cells a wing telescopes,
or a leg or antenna, every form planned

ahead of time: how many bristles,
how many facets and joints.
I click the lens into high
and move the worms around with a pin.
Their mouthparts chug, testing for something to eat.
It's coffee break in the hallway.
Someone asks about my DNA.
So far, so good, I say.

I'm a tourist in biochemistry.
The racks buzz with red-eyed flies,
haggard in their bottles.
They come with white eyes
or curly wings or extra legs, depending
on how Marcie makes the cross, how many times
you multiply four chromosomes
by each other. I look at the beakers
of clear fluid she's lined up on the windowsill
like a row of repeated skies.
I ask her, do you talk about God?

Postcards don't tell half of what the skin learns
in this latitude. I walk through it,

a beginner's course in orienteering.
Past the dry wash where we park the cars
there's a table in the shade of a palm.
Marcie grabs a compass, stubby pencil, map

marked with magnetic north. It leaves
everything out, she says. Use landmarks:
emergent, knoll, deer scat, corner of fence.
Don't worry about cattle.
No one mentions snakes, but I'm taking
what comes. Like a cactus,
my body strategizes with water.

I slap on sunblock.
Quail call from the creosote bushes.
Science is this pure.
In Sabino Canyon a spider drinks
from the only stream in miles,
a bunch of Mexican kids swing off a rope
into their birthdays.
We find the clues without guessing
how it was they got here,
using our good eyes to watch a ring of light
laid out below us in the dark like cities
or neurons or galaxies
flashing their incomplete messages in all directions.

The Many Uses of Camouflage

I got this television from my parents.
You'd be surprised, they said,
how good some of the shows are.
I don't know, sometimes
I go to the supermarket to look at
the jars of pickled eggs.

This one
is a nature show.
"To a lion, which sees the world
in shades of gray,
a zebra standing in a thicket
is only a pattern
of sunlight and trees."
I trust the narrator on this point,
since on my black and white TV
I can't see the zebra either.
The lion sprawls in the sun,
hanging her afternoon tongue out
like a rug.

It's lunchtime.
All along Main Street
women emit tiny screams.
The wind grabs their skirts,
their hair. Their makeup
beams at traffic.
It's impossible to dress
for every contingency.
The wind rising off the grassland
moves the trees, betrays
the zebra's striped rump.
It doesn't dare look round.

Downtown, young men in blue suits
blow into Tilly's with disarranged looks
and order Bloody Marys.

At last!
Pinstripes settle back
into the shapes of chairs,
and everybody's safe for once,
so long as nobody moves.

Against Maintenance

The man with the weedeater outside the door
all morning rearranging the dust
along the path, meticulously
trimming around the juniper, snipping
grass in the cracks that always grows back,
is beginning, I admit, to annoy me:
the incessant buzz of his instrument,
the rising and falling whine of a tiny motor
straining at its task of delineation.
Three times he's mown the same border,
finer gradations of sharp-edge, as near
the roots as he dares, re-proving
Zeno's claim that motion is illusion
and you can never get close enough
except in horseshoes and hand grenades,
has returned twice to the truck for intricate
cutting attachments and more gasoline
for the whirling blade, and now creeps
along with an astronaut's backpack
compressor and fat tube to blow
each severed strand and shard of sand far
far away, spic-and-spanning cement
walkways which remain oblivious
to ministrations and pebbly as the face
of the moon. Look, I admire detail
as much as the next person, it's love
that possesses the mind to squeeze perfection
from tedium, but give this man, I think,
a job he doesn't have to make stretch out
till lunch. He pauses once, framed
in my living-room window, looks over
the tops of his sunglasses in at me,
sunk under lamplight in a corner of the couch

tracing curlicues in my books, and has
the same thought. Let the grass
grow overlong, the potato vines infest
the shrubbery and dunes pile against
the screens, until we holler
we want it, rip, snort, brr-room.
Then bring heroic punctuations, curved
scimitars, and carve the world back out.
Come running. We'll strew—I promise,
we'll strew—your steps with petals.

Dissipative Structures

Two little girls standing by their bikes
in front of the Loudville store see
we're not from around here. They recommence
sorting their pooled nickels.

I unscrew my water bottle.
The poison ivy keeps me from wanting to wander.

Across the road the Manhan cascades through the woods
in midsummer flood, a speed nobody's thought up before.
We ought to be stepping across by now,
finding glued to the rocks those dry
shells of dragonfly naiads split
exactly midsection as though horror could crack
the glass between one world
and another, a metamorphosis, maybe,
but don't think you'll go anywhere like that
willingly. Last year's drought left us a path
of stones this water barely notices
except for surface punctuations,
whorls that shift while we watch, spokes
clicking backwards like a magic clock.

A girl was rearing up on a yellow horse,
purple flowered along the road. This is
how it seems now: out of its flared eye
the horse sees us pedal by, reined to its square
the way that pedestaled ballerina spun to Swan Lake
whenever I opened my jewelry box, her bright
intermittent face beating light at me like a pulsar,
on off, on off. I thought if I could switch
all the magnetic poles of my body's electrons
I'd ricochet like a bullet down a hallway,
past every door and through a pane of blue.

Something happens in the folding
of energy into matter, more than a question
of turning over in bed on a planet whizzing
like a tilt-a-whirl. This kind of blood
wasn't on schedule. You were awake too.
You said, yes. My body flushed its wayward
nosegay like a high school experiment.
It was so quiet out on the street.
Genies swarmed through the optic cables,
bearing trouble and luck like roulette.

A white-faced hornet departs his paper house
above the trash barrel. Next to the car wash,
the dog wash, the weedy restaurant emitting
the fragrance of deep-fry, the kid pumping gas
stares all day at a sign that reads MOTE.
He bends over and peels a dollar bill
off the oil patch. Inside the garage
hoses hang like fixed aortic trees.

Remember the snakes in the runoff ditch.
Remember those fourteen lady's-slippers.
Remember the baby chewing on a stick.

I know there's a place where water becomes vapor.
Witness this box of clouds.
I know how the dawn walks in.
Driving over the mountain at night,
the whole valley lies out there toward the east
like some damn circuit board,
some lovely neural wave blinking symphonically,
one naked body asleep in a safe place.
A C-5 transport floats above Westover.

Slow it down, still the film
staggers like an unbalanced table.
How long is the coast of Britain?
Didn't they decide you can't even measure it,
isthmus, bay, promontory, forking and crooking
into tiny versions of themselves,
ant worlds, microbe worlds, everybody all together
going over the mountain. I stop

midsentence, feeling back along the branches.
You can pick somewhere to stand
or you can go on, counting forever.

Travel Silk

Not all of them spin webs. The ones that do
leave them behind, except the weaving spider
who at dusk eats hers and builds all night
another in its place.
I have to keep remembering, *don't connect,*
even night comes apart on itself
in a way we begin to depend on.
Sheet, tent, orb, or dome—
each species has its own theories
about ambush. I go out to see where they've strung
chairback to bench to bottle lip.
The sun leans its light on each strand.
On darker mornings I won't know what I'm walking toward
until one brands my face, a whispered
line in space I've crossed over and survived.
I stand out in the yard under the walnut trees
and watch for hatchling silk, the thread they cast
until the wind hooks what it needs to take them off
ballooning to a farther destination. They fly
a slanted drift, as if the sun lit just one
edge of each wave passing through the air.
You turn in sleep, and when I turn
and see you through the screen,
your body folds its story out to me
the way that net of sound set up around the earth
maps out a grid for sailors lost at sea
to find their course. Here's where we are,
it says. Where do you want to go?

II
COURSE

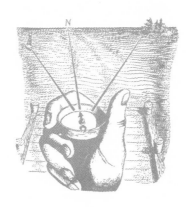

The Scout Looks for Bee Purple

Gravity's a direction
for us. Our rooms are dark,
our walls straight.

A glass falls from a hand toward
the floor, the sky is up. Light

splits to multiple
personalities, and what the bee
sees with her jeweled eye

is not our color,
though we can name it. Poppies
wave in a field of new

cups, the sweetest
drink in a bee life of looking.

Urgency brings her back
to the hive,
tracking pollen and scent

through crowded halls, meeting
the querulous clamor,
saying, look,

I'm not just dancing,
I'm showing you how

to find it: fly north-
northeast, thirty degrees
from vertical. Leave now.

Crossing New York State

The beer line's grown since Rochester.
We've been in this club car long enough
to claim our table, and our window is a movie
of backyards and wrecked fields, an endless
monotony of possibility. The ride is good.
You are trying to explain to me the desperation
of modern love. I go get us another round.
Across the wide Amtrak aisle
David and Elliot are teaching their mother
how to play War. David is losing.
He accuses Elliot of recycling his aces.
Shuffle! he screams. David and Elliot's mother
looks at us cheerfully and asks,
Are they yours?
She tips up her wine cooler,
and I begin to see what backs up to the tracks
as a ragged intimacy, den windows lit up at dusk,
the covered swimming pools, a car with one headlight
idling at the crossroad waiting to turn.
Land empties away to the west like the last tide.
You are trying to tell me what makes the vacuum
around twoness, one tiny inviolable globe,
when a voice from the back of the car interrupts
and you pause, with the face of a child
watching a coin pulled out of midair: Community,
he says, it's gone. We laugh, astonished, all of us.
The Polish student from our coach comes in
for a chicken salad sandwich. He is the reason
we are running late. He is bringing a $300 kimono
from Tokyo to his sister. We were stopped
at the border, two hours out of Toronto.
He went with one customs agent while the other
rifled his books, and freight cars loaded with broken
cement and scrap iron passed slowly on their way

---

north around the lake, the great Ontario,
the lake that could be an ocean.
I want to tell this man how the agent frowned
over his notes. I want to say, Welcome,
you are welcome here. Sit down at our table
and tell us about home. What do you study?
Will you be happy to see your sister?
And, here, eat some of our peanuts.
We were still, and it was the world out there
moving, without sound, carrying length after length,
the huge unused totality of living, like shapes
left by a metalworks: odd circles, squares, hearts.

The Fishway at Holyoke

Those industrialists knew
what the drop in the river bottom meant.
In our hands the railings hum
with sixty-five thousand
gallons per second, power
with a new personality and an old intent.
Ten minutes before each lift
crowds gather on the platform below the dam
to watch gulls stake out summer camps
in the streaked rocks
wedged with trees March snowmelt
carried over the lip and left
for the tourists like beached bones.
Lampreys struggle in musty pools,
marooned, but the shad line up in the current
thinking what we are thinking
is unlike our own minds, importantly
disengaged, discrete as a slice of pie.
When the operator starts the hydraulic gate
to shut the fish in we shout *There it goes,*
and a man explains to his young daughter.
She understands the word *want.*
She nods. She watches the gate close,
the thick links of the pulley chain
raising the metal cart filled
with smooth, dark bodies.
He says, we help them,
and as she sees the box of fish rise
toward the door of the holding tank,
she believes him.
She forgets the gulls, the gasping eels,
the rock spiders hunched in their crevices.
Water streams from the lift.

We can't see upriver from here,
the wide throat cut north past mountain hemlock,
staghorn, and combed fields edged
with blackberries, but it pulls us, it pulls
at the wasp drinking from the bowl,
the man with hair implants buying petunias
at the nursery, the woman hitching home
after two weeks in jail who says
she didn't do anything wrong, just walked
from one house to another.
The gears halt with a click and the hatch opens
and a river of fish cascades, snapping
against the I-beams, thudding on the pilings,
slipping through the space between metal and metal,
falling, and their bright sides breaking
the light into silver shards his words
try to catch for her, and he can't
remember where or how he learned
this way of measuring that keeps him
patient in the face of it,
this way of saying, honey,
most of them get in.

A Few Falls in Tuscaloosa

1. First Alabama, corner of Hackberry and Bryant

After her fenderbender
the girl at the bank weeps on and on
on the telephone. She's dialed 9 to get out
and now she's holding, longingly looking
over at the tellers, safe in their cubbies.
They punch some slips, discreetly
respecting her grief:
"Daddeee, ohhh. What do I do now?"
Out front the horrible blue lights flash,
an officer of the law stands on the grassy curb
surveying a lack of evidence—
no spilled glass, no wrenched metal.
He opens his book of forms and takes down
body language from the rear-ended party.
A chow trots by, walking a man.
The man strolls, because it's a beautiful
morning, and the blue lights are a piquant tale
he can tell his wife, whose mind
has shrunk to a walnut with a dog in it
and sometimes one other ancient, ancient shape.
The chow snuffs the cop's cuff, declines to translate.

2. Downtown Postal Station, University and 21st

She slaps her coins on the counter and wants
the pretty stamps, which they're out of,
of course.

"Look, I'm from Houston
now, where I've got an apartment, and I
came back to town to
get my stuff, but my ex-landlord's got it
all locked up, and I
need a way to get mail, but I'm homeless.
Not really, cause of
my place in Houston, but here I am. I'm
staying with Darlene,
that sweet thing from the fruit store. She lives in
Buell. Hey, they know me
at the hospital, too. I've gotten mail
there. So, could I just
make up an address? I want a box but
not for a whole six
months. I need to find this guy. He's got a
good 500 dol-
lars worth of my stuff. What do you think I
should do to get it
back? People'll screw you, you know, if you
don't watch out. Wait, is
this all the stamps I bought? All you have are
those damn little flags?"

3. Kroger's Supermarket, Northwood Plaza

Sparrows, who can live anywhere, live here
in this neon sign, in this word that's somebody's
last name. They raise their kids
wedged against the brick in the notch
between K and R in a tuft of dry stalks and straws
dangling cellophane from a pack of Lucky Strikes,
peck up their paychecks every day
from the wide asphalt apron of Wal-Mart.

You remember, there was that story

about the mud swallows,
out in Ohio someplace,

their nests torn down full
of eggs and day-old hatchlings?

It was a battle of investment strategies.
The real estate company had men and ladders,
so it won. They said it was hours
before the adults would abandon the site,
screaming around like bats long after the chicks
lay dried up in the sun like picnic scraps.

Say, it is a windy day.

You find the sturdiest
tree in the deepest part of the garden,
still it's on somebody's map.
You can just kiss that baby good-bye.

Glory over Iowa, August 1988

What you remember isn't enough to bring you
all the way back.
Intent in our rented Ford
you grope toward the turnoff, off-road
through a farmer's gate grown rusty with buttercup.
Behind us the gravel sends up a plume
in the corn. It is too dry, too hot.
It's been a long season of dust.
You have no plans, you just go
down into oaks on the Cedar's banks,
steering around the cow pats, pointing out
the cabin fronts, the swatch of blue they face.
The river's wrenched itself away from where you sat.
It's sand, a slender channel turning past,
and silt. What was it you needed to see?
The red water tower perched over town,
pink hollyhocks nodding in the alley,
an abandoned bike in the road.
You pace the drift.
Books don't mention place and time,
but that's what has to be exact.
Flying in, we saw those rings of color on the cloud,
the light that bends around the shape
of airplanes centered under sun,
and when we moved it moved with us,
we were its black, harmonic core.
I believe you when you tell me,
At night these fields can breathe.
I sift for agate quartz along the shore
and watch the shadow of a hawk blink out
the sun and cross your back.
On a hill by the old fairgrounds
silk flowers blow among the graves.
The breeze pulls zephyrs through the beans.

In Transit with Walker

You say Morocco
            looks just like Kansas.
The airstrip covers the land
        like a runner rug
            spread in the hall for strangers
who want to borrow the phone.

This week the prime minister
                makes a remark
unseemly to Saudi Arabia,
            and it's almost as hard for us
            to get out of Casablanca
as it was for Victor Lazslo.

We stand in line,
                unlikely terrorists
in running shoes, patted down
            while soldiers block the exits.
            I picture the bomb
they'll pull out of my backpack,

the red and green wires,
                the telltale
ticking. They'll find a vial
        on you, a tiny pistol, a bag
        of diamonds you can't
explain. An M16 is no metaphor,

but after lightning
                split from cumulonimbus
over New York, I'm ready for any
            destination, my body flying
            into ocean, into sleep.
Our plane crouches like a cricket.

Over the straits I practice
              an accent
on the Portuguese man in seat B.
          When the Tagus tilts into view
          he cries *Lisboa!* grabs my knee
and hangs on. No telling when

travel starts. The moment
             we walk in
that door the alleys serenade
          with household parakeets,
          the trains unwind
through olive and cork, acres

of grapes. We learn the many
             words for fish
and sit on sand in windy Viana,
          where a happy man
          in a red boat
is rowing, rowing, rowing.

Where Things Come From, Where They Go

Three benches into the park off Lincoln Street
a man in shirtsleeves smiles as he listens
to the Sox on a pocket radio. Around his feet
the moss and crabgrass advance
toward the sidewalk, and every so often the day
trots a black dog by, like the one
that follows us from the corner.
Staghorns crowd the edge of the park's steep drop,
but we can see the river fine from this height,
the four-laner bridge to South Hadley woodland
rolling over the eastern rim of the valley,
and just south the orange buoy line
warning boaters away from the dam.
Holyoke's spires and tenements step out of the Flats
toward the highway, mindful of ethnic watermarks:
Colón's Grocery, the Shamrock Cafe.
Somewhere below us a backyard goose honks,
and we go down the broken slope on our heels,
grabbing skinny trees and knocking
an avalanche of pebbles at the tracks
running up the Connecticut from New Haven
to White River Junction,
under hundreds of tunnels tattooed
with local initials and names of heavy-metal bands
and spray-painted penises faithfully rendered
and repeated magically as codes we use
to remember ourselves by.
There's a path to the slough, past storm drains
that open in the embankment like gills
leaking rusty water. The bridge breathes with pigeons.
We see bootprints in mud, a red line
of maple buds tracing highwater,
a new hatch standing in columns between trees
whose roots knee up the ground with every flood.

In August, kids swim here in their clothes,
daring each other out to stronger water
pulling hard against the pilings, then kicking
back to shore in heavy sneakers.
Late sun pours over the cliff into the cattails.
A few miles north, a slope of gray basalt
strung with monofilament and charred driftwood
slants out of water the river shallows
into steady backwards whitecaps. It goes under
the track bed and Route 5 and raises the highway
like a bear's back riding oaks and mountain laurel
and tractor trailers grinding toward Canada.
We climb the rocks and surprise two kingfishers
quarreling in piqued staccatos over water rights.
We watch a log leave shore on a long wave
and watch it return in a backwater turning
smoothed branches and bits of styrofoam clockwise.
Under the clank and creak of grackles nesting
in pines along the scrubby bank,
we find a camp of cooking pots, plastic tarps,
and blankets folded ready
at the bend the trains take slow.

Walking the Ouachita

Now I limp on, knowing
The moon strides behind me, swinging
The scimitar of the divinity
— *James Wright*

Down off the levee the houseboat marina
ties up to a provisional basin of sand,
and a black dog sniffs the decks of *Lucky Lady*,
My-T-Fine, *Ted 'n' Deb*, moored in their slots
like a floating suburb. On shore, silt

drifts in ridges around cement picnic tables
and rusted grills and heaps in an old rush
against the willow oaks. This broken road
might be the river bottom, but not now, November,
when walking the Ouachita is like trying
to break a thought cleanly in half.
I stood here waist-deep last spring,
says Bill, pointing upslope over our heads,
and now above water is no absolute.
The past blooms brown from our elbows.

Scaled with color, the river path's
a pointillist with extra paint and a feel,
like Balinese carvers, for the horror vacui.
The dog goes on ahead, marks with joy
the hull of a wrecked dingy, reappears
from the bush spiny with burrs.
-Philic, that which sticks, like
You will never understand on my father's face
as my mother names another
unreasonable tenet of Catholic faith:
plenary indulgence, she claims, is sin
insurance, deposits piled up
against a black smudge you can't wash away.

I float in the tub and consider myself
at sea level: two smooth isles
each with a perked prominence,
further a brushy delta.
The commentators quote this evidence
of the poet's growing alienation
from her own body, her self-

objectification,

or alternatively of a growing connection
to the natural, her self-

integration,

but I am really thinking of a woman
last spring who mapped me with her own fingers
from the nipple "two across and three down,"
reading from the backlit reversed-out image
of my left breast a bright dented moon.
I feel for it, remembering Wright
remembering Leopardi, "the sliver of a white
city, the barb of a jewel."

Bill gathers bouquets of burrs.
Today the radio plays
news from Yugoslavia, throats slashed in schoolrooms,
captured soldiers forced to eat
their own gouged eyes.
And myth is not a figure of speech.

When flood comes they sandbag the levee,
have parties on the second floor, and stare.
"I think it's going down!"

I want to know why I can't enter Heaven
like a visitor who relinquishes her one idea: *brink*
and begins to understand the small resistance,
the sudden blinding chute.
She's been underwater all along.

III

WAYSIDE

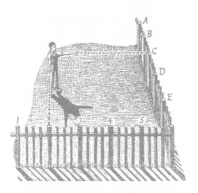

Ecumene

The V-8 engine on the floor at Reardon's
leaks a mucky clot.
The proprietor sops his coffee,
nods, Pull it up.
My car breathes hydrocarbons into a slot.

This we agree not
to acknowledge in any larger sense.

∾

It's spring. I study the shelves,
strung with belts and hoses.

The spiders this morning were lacing
scaffolds in the yew.
They'd hatched and hunkered, orange buoys backwatered
in a corner of the trellis till the weather
veered. Now a breeze rakes

the silk they climb,
the silk they spin for sails, a wild trapeze.
Put another thread on the braid.

∾

An index finger ticks off my list:
sticker, tire, taillight bulb.
Out front, someone drags in traffic.

That could bark,
the mechanic remarks, snapping in
a roller bearing
rocker box.

Invertebrate Oddities

Before changing a tire, I usually remove
my feather boa, but . . . go on, knock yourself out.
It's an interesting look.

Accomplishment is all, you were saying, hmm.
What do you do with this hooked thing?

I had a girlfriend once, incredible, really—
a brain on a cone.
She wasn't ambi or anything,
she just didn't shave.
For solidarity, I think,
or maybe she said solidity.

Anyway . . .

Solidarity, eh? I said,
like I knew what she meant.

It's not my taste.
But you, I like your propensity
to be in more than one room
and not always "at issue."

She would have given up bilateral symmetry.

See this scar?
She slugged me once with her left pump.

Here's the lug nut.

Nothing by Mouth

Susan points to the saline with her teeth in it.
She forces a grin. It's a new sensation
without incisors, saying *sixth* and *how's Steve?*
and answering the nurse's questions.
She remembers getting behind the wheel, the hill
before the curve. By the time she came to,
they'd taken Steve. He was all right.
The windshield was cracked, she could see it.

The EMTs who went back for her teeth
found them rattling around by the brake pedal.
Somebody called the car hamburger.

The woman in the next bed wants her curtain pulled.
When her family arrives they bring her the baby first.
Susan can't help herself, her tongue
keeps looking for the reliable landscape
of her mouth, going back to the holes to feel
fragments that lie in the strata.
When bulldozers cleared the lot next door to us
they hit the roots of our trees, too.
The house shivered.
The forest floor came up like scalp.

Deal

He hears the man working it, moving
down the car, the clink of coins
on coins, the sound of church,
plate traded from hand to hand,
traded back at the end of each aisle,

and remembers the square envelopes
his father licked shut every Sunday morning.
He'd see his dime reappear, a silver key
in someone's palm a continent away,
unlocking hunger, disease, exotic deaths
in countries where American money,
his father said, could buy a whole town.
Halfway through services his mother
would give him a piece of hard
candy and advice: Be good.

As far as he could tell, everyone
gave. There was enough in the plate.
Here he's not so sure how to do it.
He turns over the ace of hearts and reads,
> *Hello Im selling these*
> *cards to take care of*
> *my wife and 5 children. Please*
> *buy one. Pay any price*
> *you wish.*

The tunnels hum. Out in Cobble Hill
on the way to the F train the body shop's
erected Jesus in a box of lucite
on the roof of their garage.
Dry in weather, haloed at night
by baby spots, it watches the spare
traffic, the quotidian roadside cracks.

Something stays up late, throwing the switches.
He's begun keeping change in his pockets.
There is no choice, he thinks.
The train dips into clarity below
the riverbed, and he fishes up a warm
quarter, exacts no blessings, can't
wait for this to change his life.

The Plumber's Begun to Notice

The plumber's begun to notice how babies
meet him at every door.
The sink's clogged, the toilet runs.
Can you be here, she asks, by ten?
If he were a doctor, she'd have to
bring her faucet to him.
He arrives and there's the baby,
stoppered in.
He knows what's inside. He's got the photo
from his daughter's sonogram. A face
plain as your hand, a nose flattened
against a window. He's not sure
he should show it around.
It's a girl. He can tell from the missing
equipment. He eyes the sink, takes a wrench
to the bathroom tank.
What he won't do, he thinks, is lecture her
on maintenance. His daughter writes
she's feeling fine. She's considering marriage.
The sound's a light, she says,
that can go right through us.

The Secchi Depth

We'll measure the clarity of this lake
simply. A white disc
the size of a dessert plate

tossed overboard, descends
with resistance and give, blinks out.

You play the line,
standing with care in the boat.
Even so, the mirror ripples.

I grab the edge,
peer straight down, forgetting

the book on my knees in which I am
to be taking notes: initial
submergence, departure speed,
dread imminence of dusk.

We hear far off our wake
splash the rocks.

Not yet gone, nor returned,
more an idea than a moon, an anchor
tilted at vanishment.

The pencil skitters off deck.
I let go.

That glimmer, still.

In the Observatory

On tiptoe on the top stair
Fabio slow-dances azimuth, elevation.
The moon, pockmarked, phase-locked,
threads back through disciplined pathways
a bright dime on his cheek.

"The seeing is good tonight."

Now he swings south and hangs on
to blowzy Jupiter, sprinkled with satellites.
The scope hums, keeping time,
steady on Polaris.

In the long run gravity
is convincing.

Five stories up the astronomer
stamps his foot to illustrate
how solid we are. Compared to Jupiter,
anyway, we're a rock—
jerry-built jigsaw of tectonic
plates stuck on its nickel-iron yolk.
A very mushy egg, he says.

There's no top to this box.
We feel our way around
in red light, taking turns
with the instruments, looking out.

The metal dome revolves
medieval rumblings.
Another song starts up from some
dark branch down below:

    here

        we are here

here here

        we are

More Mere Tinkering

Einstein only wanted
to ride a ray of light.
I squat in the grass

watching you
dismember a sofa
with an axe.

The neighborhood cat
exhibits suspicion
in the asters.

When the world falls open
what is there?
Old coins, macaroni,

gum wrappers,
wonder of wonders,
a Bic lighter. Moths

fly up around your head,
thirsty, thirsty.
Hey, I know the theory

of gravitation
or I wouldn't be
standing here.

Go back to nothing,
a drowned rabbit, a bit
of purple cloth wedged

                in beechbark after flood,
that kid hard at it
                under the bridge

piling frothy chunks
                of styrofoam.
He looks up at us

                once, pulls the neck
of his T-shirt,
                weights buoyancy

with a paint can smoldering
                driftwood curls,
little boat clanking

                into the rollarcoaster
currents. Behind us
                a flicker's *kleer kleer*

rises, its scarlet nape
                torches the pines.
Now he's running

                alongside, pitching rocks
at the pyre, trying to sink it
                to see how it stops.

Chemo

The nurse comes in to say
your potassium's low, so you mug
mock horror to make us laugh.
She hooks a vial to your IV:
This may burn.
Visiting hours, we're a bunch of lieutenants
with the jitters.
You try to keep the ball rolling.
My tongue curls in my head.
All right, I'll worry about the trees
instead. Some road crew's snipped the limbs
that would have dragged ice across the wires,
thinking it was safe and cold,
too late now, pruning in December.
The sun's alive behind its glaze.
Along the street the foolish sap pearls
and drips. It fills the tiny sidewalk craters,
runs in rivered cul-de-sacs, dries the same stain
of sugar kids splash on the driveways
eating watermelon in summer.
You're thinner than I ever remember.
Like a man judging fruit for heft,
you curve your hands around your calf,
weighing memory against flesh,
this body you live in differently,
a cellar step that can't be trusted.
You show me a track from last rib past navel,
the long seam women once opened
when doctors went in gangbusters after babies,
singing, give us this little one,
this feather, this fat olive.

From you they plucked, and sewed
and said, not enough.
I follow the stories forming in your eyes.
Give us some sweet, the needles cry,
take this slivered glass, these blood
spiders, these poisoned squeezings,
we have such thirst,
please oh please, take it.

The Return of Fugitive Red

You brought a vertiginous tilt
to the room with that smile.
Something told me, put down your pencil,
this is it.

I gave up
your whole Aristotelian system
in less than a minute.
Here, take your letters, too.

When color came back
it snapped on somewhere else,
following all the laws of motion
observed by falling rocks.
My stars, I put the moves on

Tycho Brahe, who squinted at comets
long enough to see the superlunar
world was more alive
than anyone wanted.
Once that star exploded in Cassiopeia
we were onto something big.

Watch closely, correct for arc-seconds.
Now you sleep with a woman who keeps a gun
under her pillow.
I cut my hair different.
A woolly bear is starting across
the warm asphalt
no matter what we've said
about the heroic tradition.

Principia

The average man demands a faith
That answers to some scrutiny.
But philosophy cannot create a faith.

It's better meant for carving up the beast
To bite-sized bits. So as we'll see
The man, instead, demands a faith.

He pops alarming questions in his haste:
Torture—war—destruction—greed?
Philosophy cannot create the faith

He needs to keep his reservation at the feast
All day despite the wail of history.
On average, man, demand a faith!

Otherwise it seems like such a waste
To lace the planet with his bones, to be.
Bah! Philosophy cannot create a faith.

Perhaps he only wants to justify the least
Of evils on the list, i.e.,
He's average. He wants a faith.
But philosophy does not create one.

The Enthymeme in Perspective

Socrates was a man.
We know. We know
he drank the bitter cup and complained
only of cold feet, preparing to be
received by his beloved geometry.

We were all sitting there,
hands on the table in duplicate tents,
when the door blew in.

It was the rogue police,
cordoning off the area with orange tape.
They looked wildly around
and lip-synched the TV.

We have a writ!
It seemed such a dignified
death was no longer legal in this province.

My worst fear was that someone would think of
disco, but it never came to that.

They dusted his fingers for evidence,
plugged a seismograph into each orifice.

In the corner a small yellow bird with no guarantee
was singing beautifully of the life of Socrates.
The cop with the squamous face
went to make the arrest,
but the bird slipped off its feathers
and vanished, transforming the cop
to a Buddhist monk and every weapon
in the room to a pine bough.

Really, no one was surprised,
for didn't we all know the truth?

Socrates was a man.
This made him mortal.

But what of us, we then began to wonder.
What would become of us?

IV
RETURN

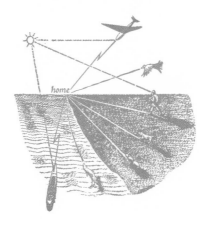

Digestion

Of all things, Classy Trojan
and Disco Mandingo come in one-two.

I blamed beginner's luck, our two-dollar bet
ballooning to eighty at the cashier's window.
You watched the bills mount in your hand
like a large vanilla Softee
demanding dexterity and appetite of us.
        I know a gift
when I see one,
but it was always your faith in something,
your iron intestines, your rapport with Cheezit-
eating seagulls.

I was looking for reasons
not to get married.

∾

Who said cold water made for firmer flesh?
He closed his fist to show the size
of abalone he'd plucked
diving off Vancouver.
He spread his fingers flat across the table.
It's a big muscle you can't chew,
      so they pound it
thin and tender into steaks.

A sudden vee of ceramic kittens
levitates toward the door.

∾

After rain the bait cups float, bonking
around the tree trunks.
                    Someone's daubed
the rocks with pink
nailpolish: FUCK YOU! 1989
also I LUV PAUL

"J. K. Russell" nicely serifed in a sandstone cliff,
southern Illinois, year of our lord April 1878.
Interstices between the stones drop
underground and stall: You are here.

I roll the last margarita around in my mouth.
Loudspeakers call out the dogs.
Two kids with T-shirts printed
                    MEGADEATH step up
and order extra sauce.

Brief History of Peacetime

The day we go to see the damaged birds
rain drapes the hills like a mist-net.
We hope what's caught lives long enough
to be let go, but we might be fooling ourselves.

Three snowy owls blink from their perches,
the great horned impassive in a tall cloak.
A rest home for raptors, I joke. A litany of injury
names the automobile as weapon of choice,

but this merlin in Habitat 5 pinwheeled
out of midwest jet exhaust, woke up here,
Woodstock, Vermont, flightless, retired.
He sells wildlife memberships at the supermarket.

The people come and go, avoiding his great sharp
eyes, dragging each other around like the dead.
The problem is not that war is so often vivid,
but that peace is so often drab. We move on.

A peregrine falcon shows off some striped trousers.
A pudgy kid appeals to high heaven: Ma, everybody
knows about the latest in attack rifles.
The sky can't clear.

The little red-tail in the next cage doesn't
get it. He shrugs his wet shoulders, crouches
over and over for takeoff, a sneeze that won't come.
We all watch that.

I've heard that trees can take lightning in,
not splitting but working the shock,
lit up inside like a pinball machine, a pitched
battle in each twig. When the tulip tree

cracked wide open and fell away
from our house, we'd forgotten any storm,
struck for once, in the middle of lunch,
by the cheap, riveting chill out there.

Double Portion Church
Letter to Michael

It just made her sad to see you
down there in the basement
wrestling with your bed of rags,
that pack of devils you refer to as growing up.
I should have told you she'd called me,
but she wasn't the only one.
She was worried. You were sleeping
next to her furnace and drinking a lot.
It wasn't that the rent was late.
It wasn't your hangdog guile
or your tendency to slippery heartrending
kindness that finally made your landlady dial
my number. This is Ellen, she claimed, as if I'd known
her all my life, and I felt that gutty
fear reserved for unexpected news
about you. But it was love, plain, human.

Perhaps I began to stutter because I'm your sister,
your best witness, the bearer of the temple truth.
Had we tried a family intervention?
I thought so. Michael, she apologized
and then she prayed in my ear. For you
she requested clarity, for me she didn't
say, but I rang off with a buzzy
slant to thought. Shouldn't I be able
to save you this time? One month later
she gets a job working construction,
on her third day is crushed to death
by a payloader. If not now, when?

I look down from the plane. Indiana
wideshot is a chaotically tiled surface

of corn, but the circuitry, the hand-stitching
on the napkins: would it be ducks or violets?
The detail goes as deep as you want.
It's not the novelist in me, it's a harder,
less dramatic science close up,
the abysmally poor hunched by the roadside
cracking rocks with hammers, a shocked
top of ocean speeding toward our continent,
and maybe you don't need to be saved, you need
to sleep it off, lunch on a rubber check,
and if you feel you have to live
this way, you do.

To Elpenor in Heaven

Homer must have known a boy like you.
The hue and cry goes up, red sails
loft in the bay, and you're up on the roof,
ankles pretzeled, rubbing wine from your eyes
and groping for a sword. Otherwise,

there's no reason for you to be in the story
at all, poor lad, blind-sided by an open manhole,
never getting near the protagonist's hat.
Over the phone, ten o'clock, a little drunk, my father
reports his results: blood test, CAT scan,
they know it's the liver. He says my liver but it.
It's in my liver. Raw from a year of chemo,
eight months clean, but the numbers, the numbers.
Talk to the big guy if you can.

To tell the truth, Elpenor,
Ulysses I could take or leave, but you—
I knew you too. Stunned outside the temple
your funeral day, I placed my hand
on the trunk of a tree and felt
the tick in my fingertips. We were young.
You left us, the basketball ponging
out of bounds, thunder in the crowd's heart,
your father down on one knee, calling, calling.

Prayer is only the right story.
The Navajo paint in sand the power of song
to change, unlock, set the moon in its swing.
So Pollen Boy sits on the sun's nose,
nine eagle feathers for each compass point,
no myth, just a kid who might be drinking
too much, trouble in the light.

This is where my life runs clear
and where my singing has to start,

where you must have heard it, in the blood
flooding the brain, the walls raining down between
    worlds.
I came halfway back from a fairy ring
to see my own enchantment lie
like ground fog all over the mountain laurel.
Tell me what to say next.

Ignis Mutat Res

The story starts with any revolution—
kelp, for example, what convinces
each pinkie-thin stem to unfurl in shafts
of brown sun its opportune flag.

Simple, a bit of a click in the works
and all gears go the other way, eagerly
spinning out the customer's new order:
sheets, the sea's curly lasagna.

Oh, it's only the genetic code, you say,
that fait accompli in multiple choice,
that conversation stopper summing up
what everybody in the room nods and hums along to,

like saying *fiscal uncertainties*
or *hegemonic doubt* or *we've grown apart,*
as if our talents in naming rivers lead them
to consult us first before flowing.

Knowing how to change is not what made us
famous, but hanging on. About adaptation
Darwin spoke statistically, I answer coolly.
You growl and hold your hands up in the air

around some shape you hope is there,
and I see unfold an accordion of windows,
six-dimensional space I might already be gone from,
out kicking a few rocks down the street.

Since last summer I can't blink away
this blind spot in my eye my doctor calls
a vitreous floater, nothing serious, too common,
especially permanent against a blank sheet

or when recounting childhood incidents.
Things start coming, and you might as well
let them. My father bends over his cancer
to stroke the dog's head. At the zoo

an elk calf struggles up off its elbows.
I'll tell the story again as though
it makes a difference. Propitiously the slime mold
assumes a sluggy complexion, migrates

an inch to the left and waves from the top
of a stalk a spore-stuffed purse,
then explodes. My love, I don't know who
resets these clocks, but not us.

The Law of Similars

The way I saw it was, go in after those plums,
yank any hydra-head up by the stem.
All the same, then, you have to listen
to the dead tell their stories,
palming no antidote except your own language.

You can use it to name your babies.
You can use it wherever, my dearest,
mi cielo, mon amour, o tall man of stars
reclining on wintry hills.
You can shock us with cheap juxtapositions.
For example, list three species of torture:

Nine-joints
Devil's nettle
Man-under-ground,

night-blooming, poison-sweet.

"I took a tape recorder around for a while.
I went into a nuclear power plant once.
But the best sound there came from a little fan
someone had stuck up over a desk.
A random kind of squeak. I collected it.
I thought it might come in useful."

The homeopathic magicians worked by analogy, too,
like Frazer says, out in the fields all day
ransacking nature for clues: To be cured
of jaundice, draw a deep stare
from the yellow eye of a stone-curlew.

Bottled arsenal of apothecary jars,
monkshood, calendula, honeybee corpse
floating in dilution—oh, poets, you wish!
Utility bill, movie ticket, curled leaf,
alchemical library of language or bust,
you're any stranger mooching directions,
a woman waiting for blueprints:

"My staircases. I build them all over the house,
floor to ceiling. They go nowhere, but the ghosts tell me
they need them. So I do it."

You just listen and you know you're underdressed,
nobody to pal around with like Athena or Coyote,
the shape-changers, intelligent powers of light
you can lay no claim to. Amen. Shantih, shantih.

Whispers antiphonal. A random kind of squeak.
I collected it.
I thought it might come in useful.

THE
JUNIPER
PRIZE

This volume is the twenty-fourth recipient of the Juniper Prize
presented annually by the University of Massachusetts Press
for a volume of original poetry.

The prize is named in honor of Robert Francis,
who lived for many years at Fort Juniper,
Amherst, Massachusetts.